HORRID HENRY

UP, UP AND AWAY

FRANCESCA SIMON

ILLUSTRATED BY TONY ROSS

Orion

**For Christina Lamb, fearless journalist,
heroic water-slide comrade**

ORION CHILDREN'S BOOKS

This book first published in Great Britain in 2019
by Hodder and Stoughton

1 3 5 7 9 10 8 6 4 2

Text © Francesca Simon 2019
Illustrations © Tony Ross 2019
Additional images © Shutterstock

The rights of Francesca Simon and Tony Ross to be identified as author and
illustrator of this work have been asserted.

A CIP catalogue record for this book is available from the British Library.

ISBN 978 1 5101 0592 8

Printed and bound in Great Britain by Clays Ltd, Elcograf S.P.A.

The paper and board used in this book are from well-managed forests and other
responsible sources.

www.hachettechildrens.co.uk
www.horridhenry.co.uk

CONTENTS

MEET THE

200 CM

175 CM

150 CM

HENRY

PETER

125 CM

100 CM

75 CM

50 CM

25 CM

0 CM

GANG

MUM AND DAD

MARGARET

RALPH

HORRID
HENRY

UP, UP AND AWAY

oh wow! **Oh wow!
Oh boy oh boy oh boy!**
Horrid Henry could scarcely
believe it. After years of him BEGGING
and pleading and pleading and BEGGING,
Horrid Henry's mean, **HORRIBLE**
parents were finally taking him on
an *aeroplane*. It was a dream
come true.

Mum and Dad's idea of a great
holiday was staying at home and
weeding the garden. Or **WORSE**,
forcing **HIM** to help weed the garden.
Or **EVEN WORSE**, camping in a SMELLY

mosquito-filled swamp without TV or computers or **ANYTHING**.

GAG. **BLECCCCCCCCCH**.

YUCK.

These weren't holidays.

These were organised **CRUELTY** to children. One happy day, when Henry was **KING**, he'd make sure that kids decided where to go on holiday, and any parent who so much as *whispered* the words **GARDEN** or **CAMPING** or **FRESH AIR** would get **trampled** by stampeding penguins.

But now, at last, they were flying off on a real vacation, to stay in a hotel with twelve **HUGE** pools, wave machines and room service and **EVERYTHING**. It was like taking a holiday in *heaven*.

Horrid Henry had never flown on an aeroplane. But he knew all about it. Stuck-up Steve had bragged about the flight he and Rich Aunt Ruby had just taken. Your own cabin complete with baskets filled with *chocolates* and **CRISPS**. *Luxury* beds.

Flight stewards at your beck and call
whenever you wanted more sweets
or an extra burger – OR THREE.
Non-stop **ice cream** and FIZZYWIZZ
drinks and TV and games. Any food
you liked, brought to you with a
SNAP of your fingers as you reclined
in your fabulous **comfy** chair.
Horrid Henry couldn't wait to be
soaring through the air, watching
every episode of *Terminator
Gladiator* or *Skeleton Skunk*, a
huge bowl of *chocolates* by his side.
Best of all, his parents couldn't

nag him to do his chores, finish his homework or turn off the TV. Not on a plane. He'd be *FREE*.

In fact, maybe he could fly the plane. How hard could it be? He could ride a bike. Maybe he could do a few *loop the loops* while he was *SOARING* through the clouds. **Pilot Henry**. With an **EJECTOR SEAT** for his younger brother, Perfect Peter.

But would the flight be long enough to play **EVERY** game and watch **EVERY** episode? Henry hoped so. He couldn't wait to relax in his own *mini-palace* in the sky.

The only bad thing was that for some reason his

NAPPY NOODLE

wormy worm

wibble wobble

POOPY PANTS

POOPSICLE

brother was coming too, instead of being put out with the recycling.

Horrid Henry SCOWLED. He couldn't wait to **SLAM** the door shut on his private cabin so he wouldn't have to see the **TOADY TOAD** for the whole flight.

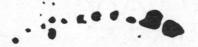

At last the great day arrived. After *checking* they had tickets and passports, and then *double-checking* they had tickets and passports, and then *triple-checking* they had

tickets and passports, Henry, Peter, Mum and Dad finally arrived at the airport.

"**Out of my way, worms!**" shrieked **Horrid Henry**, **ZOOMING** to the departure gate on his Marvin the Maniac Glidy-Glidy wheeled suitcase, **CRASHING** into people and **KNOCKING** over duty-free displays. "I've got a plane to catch."

"Don't be **HORRID**, Henry!"
shouted Mum.

"HENRY, GET BACK HERE!"
shouted Dad.

But **Horrid Henry** ignored them.
Why queue when paradise beckoned?
He'd already wasted *so* much time
WAITING in line to check in, **WAITING** in
line for security, **WAITING** in line to **WAIT**
in line. Horrid Henry couldn't **WAIT**
another **second**.

He ran ahead and jumped on to
the jet, *pushing* and **SHOVING** past
everyone waiting to board. He had to

make sure he got a window seat.
He dashed through the plane door
and stared. **OOH! Yes! Oh wow!**
Stuck-up Steve had been telling
the truth.

There were the **HUGE** reclining
seats, with the **MASSIVE** TVs and
fluffy pillows.

And, even better, there were plenty
which were still empty. Henry raced
to bag one by the window.

Horrid Henry sank into the
leather chair. It was **MASSIVE**.
There was the basket filled with

chocolates and **CRISPS**. The bell to call the flight attendant. Or should he say, his own personal butler.

And best of all, a **GINORMOUS** TV screen all for him. Just look at all the channels on the remote control. Horrid Henry's thumbs *itched* to get started.

It was even better than he'd hoped.

But for some reason Horrid Henry's parents didn't rush to bag their own *mini-palace*. Instead, they stood in the aisle with Peter, **GLARING** at him.

"Hurry up," said Henry. "Or you won't get a seat."

"Henry," said Dad. "We're not sitting here."

"Yeah, Henry," said Peter.

WHAT? Were they ~~CRAZY?~~ Was there somewhere even better? Maybe with a **swimming pool** and a *ski slope?*

"This is first class," said Mum.

"So?" said Henry, scooping up a fistful of sweets.

A flight attendant walked towards them, smiling.

"*Hello! Welcome on board. I'm Greg, here to*

make your flight a great one."

Then Greg caught sight of Henry's ticket. His smile vanished. He grabbed the sweets out of Henry's hand.

"**Oi**," said Horrid Henry. "**GIVE THOSE BACK**."

"Move," said Grumpy Greg. "**AND MAKE IT SNAPPY**."

"But I like it here," said Henry.

He held on to the plush armrests.

"Get up **NOW** or there will be **NO TV** during the flight," *hissed* Mum.

Reluctantly, Henry got out of his KING-SIZE seat.

Where they were going had better be good, he thought, **SCOWLING**, as he followed his parents down the aisle and through the curtain.

A gruesome sight met his eyes.

"**STOP!** Let's go back," protested Henry.

Henry's parents ignored him

and carried on walking.

DOWN, DOWN, DOWN they trudged, towards the back of the plane.

The seats got **smaller** and **smaller** and smaller. The aisles got NARROWER and NARROWER and NARROWER. Henry looked in horror at the cramped rows.

"TURN BACK. TURN BACK. WHY ARE WE GOING HERE?" he shouted.

Mum, Dad and Peter ignored him, and continued SQUEEZING down the tiny aisle to the second to last row of seats in the middle by the TOILETS.

"Here," said Dad.

"This is nice and cosy," said Peter.

Horrid Henry was so shocked
he couldn't move. Was this some
CRUEL joke? Had he been *zapped*
into the **ZOMBIE** dimension? These
postage stamp seats weren't even by
a window.

"I CAN'T SIT HERE!" screamed
Horrid Henry. "I'll suffocate."

"Sit down," ordered Grumpy Greg.
He clicked his fingers. "And make it
SNAPPY. You're blocking the aisle."

Reluctantly, Horrid Henry **HEAVED**

himself into his teeny tiny **lumpy bumpy** seat.

Dad **SQUEEZED** into his tiny seat.

Mum **SQUEEZED** into her tiny seat.

Peter **SQUEEZED** into his tiny seat.

"The holiday starts here," said Dad cheerfully. "Buckle up."

Across the aisle a red-faced baby
began to howl.

"WAAAAAAAHHHH!"
And another.

"WAAAAAAAAAHHHH."
And another.

"WAAAAAAAAHHHHH."
Then Horrid Henry saw a
terrible sight.

"**WHERE'S MY TV?**" he wailed,
kicking and hurling
himself
backwards
in the seat.

"**OWWWWW**," yelped the man sitting in front of him.

"**OWWWWW**," yelped the woman sitting behind him.

"**WHERE'S MY TV?**" bellowed Henry again.

"I guess they don't have them back here," said Mum.

"You can read a book," said Dad.

"I've brought loads of books," said Peter. "You can borrow some of mine. I've got THE HAPPY NAPPY, BUNNY'S BEST HOLIDAY, KITTEN'S MITTEN—"

"**NO!**" howled Henry. "I want to

watch TV. I want to play games."

Horrid Henry

kicked the seat as

hard as he could,

then *FLUNG*

himself backwards

as **FEROCIOUSLY**

as he could.

"AAAARRRGGGHH,"

yelped the man in front again.

He stood up. Orange juice

dripped down his shirt. "You

made me spill my drink.

I'm soaked."

"**AAAARRRGGGHH**," yelped the woman behind him. She stood up. Coffee **dripped** down her jumper. "You made me spill my drink too."

Too late, **HOrrid HenrY** remembered an extra bit of Steve's bragging.

"Of course YOU'LL be flying economy," Stuck-up Steve had said.

"No I won't." Horrid Henry hadn't known what economy was. But now, unfortunately, he did.

The plane took off. The babies howled. Henry **kicked**.

"**ARRRRRRGGGH**," yelled the man in front. He stood up. Tomato juice **DRIBBLED** down his face onto his shirt. "Stop **kicking** me!"

"Don't be **horrid**, Henry!" shouted Mum.

Mum read her book.

Dad read his book.

Peter read his book.

Horrid Henry **kicked**
the seat in front.

"**Beef burger**,
chicken, or VEGETABLE
BAKE WITH SPROUTS?" asked
Chirpy Cheryl, making her way slowly
down the aisle with her trolley.

"**Beef burger**? *Chicken*?
VEGETABLE BAKE?"

Henry's tummy RUMBLED.

At least there were **burgers**.

"I want a **burger**," said Henry, when Cheryl eventually reached their row.

"We've only got VEGETABLE BAKE WITH SPROUTS left," said Chirpy Cheryl.

"Oh yum," said Perfect Peter, as green sludge was SLOPPED onto his tray table.

"What happened to the **burgers**?" wailed Horrid Henry.

"Gone," said Chirpy Cheryl.

GONE?

Was there no end to the misery he was enduring?

No TV. No burger.

Squished into a seat that would crush a grasshopper.

A huge queue for the smelly toilets. Screaming babies.

Horrid Henry kicked the seat as hard as he could.

"AAARRRGGHH!" yelped the man in front. He stood up. Vegetable bake dripped down his hair on to his clothes.

SNORE SNORE.

SNORE SNORE.

Mum was SNORING.

Dad was SNORING.

Perfect Peter was SNORING.

Horrid Henry was STARVING.

KICK KICK

KICK

THUNK THUNK

THUNK

"**ARRRRRRGGGH!**" yelped the man in front. "**MY TEA!**"

"**ARRRRRRGGGH!**" yelped the woman behind. "**MY COFFEE!**"

"*Wah!*" a baby wailed.

Another joined in.

"*Wah!*"

And another.

"*WAAAAHHHH!*"

Horrid Henry could stand it no longer. He'd go mad if he stayed in this HELLHOLE. Unless he starved to death first. When Mum and Dad woke up, they'd find a shrivelled bag

of bones in his seat. Then they'd be sorry. But it would be too late.

Goodbye, cruel world, thought Henry.

And then Horrid Henry had a brilliant, SPECTACULAR idea. Why hadn't he thought of it before? He didn't have to put up with this torture. He didn't have to starve or shrivel into a mummy.

Horrid Henry checked up the aisle.

Horrid Henry checked down the aisle.

The coast was clear.

He **SQUEEZED** past snoring Mum. Then *quick* as he could, he ran up to the front and *slipped* under the curtain and into first class.

There were loads of empty seats waiting for him.

Horrid Henry nabbed one by the window. He *stretched* out his aching legs and **GRABBED** the remote. Then he **SNATCHED** a bar of *chocolate* and stuffed it in his mouth.

Ahh. This was where he belonged. The lap of luxury. Peace at last.

A **DARK SHADOW** fell over him.

"**OI!** That's not your seat. Get back where you belong and **MAKE IT SNAPPY**," snapped Grumpy Greg.

"**NO!**" shrieked Horrid Henry. "**NOOOOOOO!**" They'd have to drag him away.

A long-haired man, dozing under a hat across the aisle, looked up. He stared at Henry.

"So sorry to disturb you, sir," said Grumpy Greg. "He'll be removed **immediately**."

"Henry? Is that you?" asked the

long-haired man.

It was **KING KILLER**, lead singer of the **KILLER BOY RATS**, Henry's favourite band. Henry had met him backstage when **KING KILLER** had invited Henry to be his guest at the **MANIC PANIC** concert.

"**KING!**" said Horrid Henry.

"Great to see you, Henry," said **KING KILLER**.

"Get back to your seat," ordered Grumpy Greg. "And make it **SNAPPY.**"

"It's OK," said **KING KILLER**. "He's with the band."

"Gonna be a rock star . . . and you ain't!" **Horrid Henry** hummed his favourite Killer Boy Rats song as he popped another *chocolate* into his mouth. Decisions, decisions. Another

burger, or more *cake*? Another episode of *Terminator Gladiator*, or should he change channels to *Marvin the Maniac*? More **CRISPS**? More *ice cream*?

"Oh steward," said Horrid Henry, "bring me some more chocolate cake and . . . make it snappy!"

HORRID HENRY

CHANGES HISTORY

Blabby blabby **blabby blabby** blabby. **Blah** blah **blah** blah **blah**. History **blah**. Tudor **blah**.

Henry VIII **BLAH**.

MISS BATTLE-AXE droned **ON** and **ON** and **ON**. What was she spluttering about now?

Horrid Henry lent her an ear.

Oh. She was still blabbing about that old king and his stupid wives.

Horrid Henry withdrew his ear. Back to imagining he was saving planet Earth from the intergalactic

47

SLIME MONSTERS by squirting them with **super-duper goo** from his super-powerful Goo-Shooter.

SPLAT! *SQUISH!* **SQUASH!**

The alien slime monster captain was covered in goo. Yes! She tried to fire back but hurrah — her laser jammed. It was filled with goo! Yes! *Superhero Heroic Henry* had done it again. He'd saved the world. All the slimy alien could do was squeak while grateful earthlings cheered and chanted his name.

"Henry! Henry! **HENRY!!!!**"

48

Heroic Henry
looked up.

The **ALIEN SLIME MONSTER** was glaring down at him with her **bulging** red eyes and **SHARP** yellow teeth.

"I said, how many wives did King Henry VIII have?" said Miss Battle-Axe.

How was he supposed to know? thought Horrid Henry. Who knew that sort of useless fact?

"I'm waiting," said **MISS BATTLE-AXE**,

FIRE escaping from her nostrils.

"I know, I know," shouted **Moody Margaret**, waving her hand.

Must have been more than one, thought Henry. But somehow he didn't think two was the right answer.

"Nineteen?" guessed **Horrid Henry**.

"Thirty-two!" yelled Rude Ralph.

"**SIX. HE HAD SIX**," shrieked Margaret, sticking her tongue out at Henry.

"And I can name them all," said Clever Clare. "Catherine. Anne. Jane.

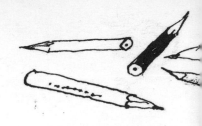

Anne. Catherine. Katherine."

"Divorced. Beheaded. Died.
Divorced. Beheaded. Survived," said
Miss Battle-Axe. "Well done, Clare."

Too bad that batty old **horrid
Henry VIII** hadn't married
MISS BATTLE-AXE instead of all those
Catherines and Annes, thought
Henry. If **MISS BATTLE-AXE** had got hold
of that king, she'd have *chopped off*
his head. That would have taught
him to stop changing wives and
boring children of the future with
all those names to learn.

Anyway, who cared how many wives **KING GREEDY GUTS** had? If only Henry had been in charge, he'd have made sure Henry VIII had **NO WIVES**.

MISS BATTLE-AXE scowled at her class. One day she'd take a rocket to the moon, open a café there and eat buns all day. But until that happy moment . . .

"I have an exciting announcement," said **MISS BATTLE-AXE**. "I want everyone to write at least four pages about living in Tudor times for our class

essay competition. The competition will be judged by **Mrs Oddbod**."

Competition? Competition? A competition meant *prizes!* Horrid Henry loved prizes.

"What's the prize?" shouted Horrid Henry.

"The best prize of all — satisfaction for a job well done," said **MISS BATTLE-AXE**. "And of course, the chance to represent our school in the nationwide history quiz."

Boo. Horrid Henry **SLUMPED** in his seat.

That wasn't a prize. A prize was winning your weight in *chocolate*. Or a lifetime supply of *ice cream*. Trust birdbrain **MISS BATTLE-AXE** to think that doing a history quiz was a prize. Well, there was no danger of his winning. Horrid Henry knew almost NOTHING about the Tudors.

He'd scribble down some RUBBISH as fast as he could, then get back to doing something important – reading the brand-new SCREAMIN' DEMON comic he'd hidden under his desk.

Horrid Henry picked up his

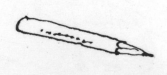

pencil. He wasn't wasting his
valuable comic-reading time writing
four pages, that was for sure.

What a horrible thought, living in
Tudor times.

TUDOR TIMES
_____

SO SMELLY.
SO BORING.
YUCK.

THE END

Done! SCREAMIN' DEMON here I come.
Horrid Henry flung down his pencil

and opened his comic.

Oh, that Demon was playing with fire this time. Would he—

Yank! A horrible **bony** hand snatched his paper off his desk.

"**EVERYONE** must take part in the essay competition or there will be **NO** playtime today," snarled Miss Battle-Axe, **GLARING** at him and crossing out "THE END". "And that means writing **AT LEAST** four pages."

Horrid Henry gasped. No playtime? That was a **FATE WORSE THAN DEATH.**

He had no choice but to *spew* out four pages. But *why oh why* did he have to write a history essay? Why couldn't he write a story about blasting **SPACE MONSTERS?** Or fighting **SKELETON PIRATES?** Now that would be interesting.

Horrid Henry picked up his
heavy pencil again. He wrote:

History. There's far too much of it. If only
I'd been alive in the past to stop history,
everything would be a lot better, and children
would have loads more time to watch telly and
eat crisps.

Take William the Conqueror. If I'd been
there, I'd have ambushed William with my Goo-
Shooter. He'd never have made it off the boat.
He'd be William the No-Conqueror.

Then there would be **NO HISTORY** to torture
students of the future. And everyone would

have lived happily ever after.

But unfortunately, I wasn't around then to save the day. Which is why we have to learn about living in Tudor times, which were **REALLY DULL**. Everyone just walked around yawning because there was nothing to do. **NO TELLY. NO COMPUTERS.** You had to wear big ruffs round your neck and prance around in **SILLY SHOES** and try not to die of boredom. Which was very hard. That's why everyone **DIED** so often.

Because there was no telly you had to go and see one of Shakespeare's long boring plays

where characters say things like "To be or not to be". Well, I say **NOT TO BE**. If I'd been there to save the day, Shakespeare would be banished to a desert island for his crimes against children of the future.

Horrid Henry put down his pencil. He was **EXHAUSTED**. He needed to write more but that was all the Tudor history he knew. He'd been fighting *INTERGALACTIC SPACE MONSTERS* while Miss Battle-Axe had been jabbering on about **TUDOR THIS** and **TUDOR THAT**.

Henry looked around. Everyone else was scribbling away while he'd barely written two pages.

Even **Beefy Bert** was writing loads.

Horrid Henry sneaked a peek at Bert's paper. Maybe he could copy him.

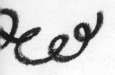

Bert had written:

I dunno.
I dunno.
I dunno.

Great, thought Henry. Just great.
Clever Clare was sitting in front of
him. Craning his neck, Henry could
see she was already on page eight.
If he moved his chair JUST A FRACTION to
the right, he could see a bit of Clare's
essay. Maybe he could copy her.

Sir Walter Raleigh brought back potatoes from the New World in 1587. His children were named Carew, Damerei and Walter. Queen Elizabeth I liked him very much, until she discovered that he had . . .

Henry *stretched* and **STRAINED** but he couldn't see any more.

He was on his own.

Sighing, he continued scribbling.

Walking down a smelly Tudor street, you were sure to meet Sir Walter Raleigh carrying a big sack of potatoes. He'd be with his children, who were crying because they had such weird Tudor

names: Carew and Damerei. Sir Walter was crying too, because Queen Elizabeth didn't like him any more, after she discovered he had ...

He had what? wondered Henry. Robbed a bank? Stuck his tongue out at her? *Farted?*

... after she discovered he had **BAD BREATH.**

Unfortunately, you would also meet Henry VIII followed by his **SIX WIVES.** If you could, you would cross the road fast because he liked chopping off Tudor heads. You were especially

in danger if your name was **CATHERINE** or **ANNE**. *Another reason why living in Tudor times was so* **TERRIBLE.**

Hmmm. Well, at least he'd used the word *Tudor* loads. Did he know any other bits of history he could

stuff into his essay to make it up to four pages? Even if it wasn't about the Tudors, no one could complain it wasn't about history.

Here are a few more important history facts everyone should know.

The **BLACK DEATH** was even worse than the **PINK DEATH** or the **YELLOW DEATH**. And don't get me started on the **GREEN DEATH**. Like I said, there was lots of death in history. Which is another reason why **HISTORY IS HORRIBLE**.

Before the Tudors, there were cavemen.

They had their own kings, like **KING CLUBHEAD** and **KING STONEFACE**. They liked fighting dinosaurs, which is why dinosaurs are extinct, otherwise that **horrid King Henry VIII** would have hunted them. Come to think of it, a **T. REX** would have hunted him for a tasty snack.

Hurrah. He'd managed to write nearly four pages. A few more sentences and he'd be done.

SCREAMIN' DEMON comic here I come, thought Horrid Henry as he filled up the final page with the **biggest** handwriting he could.

It's much better to be alive today than in Tudor times. Or in the bad old olden days when history was starting.

THE END

"Time's up," said **MISS BATTLE-AXE**, collecting the papers.

That was the perfect essay, thought **Horrid Henry**. No way he'd win, but no one could say he hadn't tried. He opened his comic and sighed happily. Just a few more minutes till playtime.

The next morning the head, *Mrs Oddbod*, came into the classroom, holding a thick folder. She whispered to Miss Battle-Axe. **MISS BATTLE-AXE** went green.

"What do you mean, I gave out the **WRONG** topic?" she spluttered. "They weren't meant to write about the Tudors?"

"That's for next year," said *Mrs Oddbod*. "They were supposed to write about *Great Moments in History*."

MISS BATTLE-AXE sat down and wiped her brow. In thirty-five years of teaching she had never made a mistake. Maybe it was time to think about running away and joining an expedition to the South Pole.

Mrs Oddbod stood in front of the class.

"The bad news is that you were accidentally given the **WRONG TOPIC** for the essay competition."

Clever Clare burst into tears. *Brainy Brian* looked faint.

"The *good* news, however, is that one person seems to have written partly about the right topic. A very . . . ERRR . . . interesting response.

"So I am pleased to tell you that our school will be represented at the nationwide history quiz by . . . Henry."

WHAT?

HUH?

"Congratulations, Henry. We will start our history quiz preparations immediately. See me every day after school for extra practice."

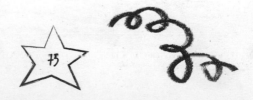

Mrs Oddbod dumped a load of books on his desk.

BIG BOOKS.

Fat books.

Dusty books.

What? What?

"NOOOOOOOOOOOOOOOOO!"

HORRID
HENRY
STEALS THE
SHOW

"How many badges do you have, Henry?" asked Perfect Peter.

"Tons," said **Horrid Henry**. "Now out of my way, worm, I'm busy." He'd just got hold of the latest **SKELETON SKUNK AND THE WIZARD OF WONDER** story and was desperately trying to finish it before Dad started **NAGGING** him to do his homework.

"I already have ten badges," said Perfect Peter. "That's five more than I need to go on the school trip to **WILD WATER-SLIDE PARK**."

"Bully for you," said Horrid Henry.

"You know that tomorrow is the deadline to earn all your badges," said Peter.

Horrid Henry stopped reading.

WHAT? **WHAT?**

That was IMPOSSIBLE.

He had weeks and weeks and weeks left to get those *stupid* badges. Hadn't he already signed up to do the sound effects for Miss Battle-Axe's dreadful school play, *THE GOOD FOOD FAIRY*, just so he could earn his Entertainer badge?

And now he had to earn **FOUR** more? **BY TOMORROW?**

It was so unfair.

But there was no time to lose if he wanted to race down the **ZOOM OF DOOM**, the most **TERRIFYING** water slide in the universe, or **Belly Flop Drop**, or all the other BRILLIANT, *amazing*, **FANTASTIC** rides at the best water-slide rollercoaster park in the WHOLE WIDE WORLD. Horrid Henry had always wanted to go. But his mean **horrible** parents would never take him.

Horrid Henry pushed past Peter, dashed to his bedroom and grabbed the Badge Sheet he'd been given ages ago from under a pile of DIRTY SOCKS and MUDDY JEANS. Frantically, he skimmed it, searching for the *quickest*, **easiest** badges to earn.

Why did so many badges involve hard work? Ugh. Where was the TV-WATCHING BADGE when he needed it?

Horrid Henry scanned the list. Let's see, let's see — *Take Care of an Animal* badge. He took care of FAT Fluffy, didn't he, by letting him sleep all the time. Oh wait. *Look after an animal for two months.* Henry

didn't have two months, he had
one night.

Hiking badge? No way. Horrid
Henry **SHUDDERED**. Too dangerous.
RAMPAGING CHICKENS, **MARAUDING
VAMPIRES** — who knew what horrible
monsters were waiting just to nab
him as he *heaved* his heavy bones?

What a shame he'd been disqualified from earning the *Giving Good Advice* badge after *Vain Violet* had asked: *"How can I be more beautiful?"* and Henry had replied, **"change your head."**

Wait. Wait.

A *Cooking* badge.

YES YES YES!

"I'm cooking tonight," shouted Horrid Henry.

"I'm cooking tonight," said Perfect Peter. "I want to get another badge ..."

Horrid Henry marched into Peter's

bedroom, grabbed Peter's favourite sheep, Fluff Puff, and DANGLED it over the loo.

"Who's cooking tonight?" said **Horrid Henry.**

"You are," wailed Peter.

Mum stared at the pile of **CRISPS** on her plate.

Dad stared at the pile of **CRISPS** on his plate.

Peter stared at the pile of **CRISPS** on his plate.

"Eat up," said Horrid Henry, stuffing **CRISPS** into his mouth. "There's seconds."

"Why are we eating **CRISPS** for dinner?" said Dad.

"It's the first course of your two-course meal so I can earn my *Cooking* badge," said Henry. "I have to include two vegetables. **OVEN CHIPS** with **ketchup** coming up."

"This is **NOT** healthy eating," said Mum.

"Is too," said Horrid Henry. "**Ketchup** is a vegetable, which is why it's called **tomato** ketchup. **CHIPS** and **CRISPS** are made from potatoes. And I've already done the different ways to prepare and cook food part."

Hadn't he *ordered* a pizza this month? *Tick*. **Microwaved** a burger? *Tick*. And *taken the wrapper off* a chocolate bar? *Tick tick tick.* That *Cooking* badge was his.

Dad ate a handful of **CRISPS** and then patted his stomach. "I shouldn't really, I need to banish my belly," he said. "All my trousers are getting tight."

"So stop eating, **fatso**," said Horrid Henry.

"Don't be **horrid**, Henry!" said Mum.

"I'm not being **horrid**," said Henry. "I'm earning my *Handy Helper* badge by helping Dad banish his belly. So please can you sign my form? About how considerate and caring I am?"

"**NO**," said Mum.

"**NO**," said Dad.

"**ARRRRGGGGHHH!**" wailed Horrid Henry. "I need the badges **NOW**."

"You have to earn badges," said Perfect Peter.

"Quite right, Peter," said Mum.

Horrid Henry scowled. Here he was, working his **guts** off to earn badges, and his **MEAN**, **horrible** parents were being **MEAN** and **horrible.**

And as for his *wormy worm* brother . . .

"Mum, Dad, listen to the song I wrote," said Henry. "It's for my **Write and Sing a Song** badge."

Horrid Henry leapt on to a chair and started to sing.

"PETER IS A **POOP POOP POOPSICLE.**
NO ONE IS A **WORMIER WORM.**
HE'S A **NINNY** AND A **MINI**
SHOULD BE THROWN INTO A **BIN-i,**
HE'S A **POOP POOP POOP POOP POOPSICLE.**"

"Mum!" wailed Peter. "Henry called me a poopsicle."

"That's a TERRIBLE song, Henry," said Dad.

"No it isn't," said Henry. "It rhymes. And I wrote it myself. Where does it say it has to be a nice song?"

"Henry . . ." said Mum.

"Oh all right," said Horrid Henry.

"I'll sing one more." If only there was a **PARENT SWAP** badge . . .

"HENRY IS THE TOP
HENRY IS THE BEST.
YOU DON'T EVEN NEED
TO PUT IT TO THE TEST.

MARGARET IS A FROG-FACE
SHE'S A DISGRACE.
I WISH SHE'D BLAST OFF

INTO OUTER SPACE —
NO! HYPER-SPACE!
THEN I'D NEVER HAVE TO SEE
THAT FROGGY FROGGY
FROG-FACE AGAIN.
RIBBIT."

Dad signed for the **Write and Sing a Song** badge.

Mum signed for the *Cooking* badge.

Dad signed for the *Handy Helper* badge but only on condition that Henry set and cleared the table for a month.

Three badges down. The fourth, the **Entertainer** badge, would be his tomorrow. Then, just one more to get.

The **COLLECTOR** badge! Of course. Didn't he collect gizmos? And comics? Yes he did.

TICK.

There was one last requirement to get that badge. *Talk about someone else's collection.*

"I hate your sheep collection, Peter!" bellowed Horrid Henry.

TICK.

He'd earned the *Cooking* badge, the *Handy Helper* badge, the **Write and Sing a Song** badge and the **COLLECTOR** badge.

Just one more badge and it's WATERPARK HERE I COME, thought

Henry. All he had to do was the sound effects for **MISS BATTLE-AXE'S TERRIBLE** play tomorrow, and he'd be *whizzing* down the **ZOOM OF DOOM** in no time.

Horrid Henry sat backstage with the sound board on a table in front of him. All the buttons were labelled:

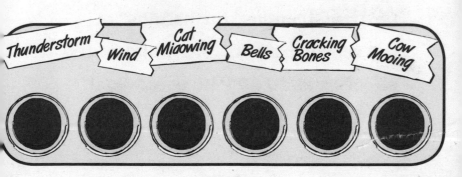

The second row sounds were:

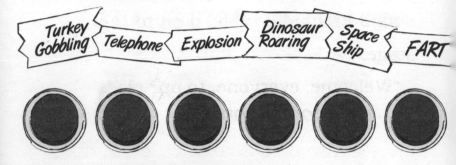

Turkey Gobbling | Telephone | Explosion | Dinosaur Roaring | Space Ship | FART

"**DO NOT TOUCH** the second row," hissed **MISS BATTLE-AXE**. "Every sound you need for this play is in the **TOP ROW**. Do exactly what we rehearsed."

Horrid Henry scowled. Naturally, he'd read comics during most of the rehearsals, but providing sound effects was *so easy* he could do it

94

in his sleep.

MISS BATTLE-AXE walked on to the stage.

"Welcome, everyone, to our class play, *THE GOOD FOOD FAIRY*, written by me. I'm also delighted to welcome the theatre critic from our local paper. We look forward to his review of our show."

The auditorium lights dimmed. SOUR SUSAN appeared, dressed in black.

"IT WAS A DARK AND STORMY NIGHT," said Susan. Henry pressed the THUNDERSTORM button.

BANG! BANG! BANG! BOOM! BOOM! BOOM!

"THE WIND WAS HOWLING —" Horrid Henry pressed the *Wind* button — *Whoooooooooo* — "and snow was falling on poor, hungry Tiny Tim."

Brainy Brian sat cross-legged on stage, holding a crutch and shivering, as **ANXIOUS ANDREW** emptied a bucket of paper snow on him.

"What a **TERRIBLE** Victorian night," said Tiny Tim. "I wonder what's for supper? Wouldn't it be great to have a nice **plump** roast turkey? Oh no! **GRUEL** again! How I wish I had some fresh food like broccoli to eat. Or string beans, or tomatoes, or apples. If only I could travel to the future and enjoy a healthy meal.

"But hark! What's that I hear? It must be the *Good Food Fairy*, coming to visit."

Ding-a-ling! Ding-a-ling. Henry chimed the fairy bells as Moody Margaret swept on to the stage.

"Hello, poor person from the past," said Margaret. She waved her wand. "I've come to grant your wish. Let me show you the *wonderful* food of the future.

"First, drink *milk* and eat **cheese** for strong bones. You don't want your bones to break —"

CRUNCH CRACK
CRUNCH CRACK

"— because you haven't eaten enough calcium."

Margaret the *Good Food Fairy* continued **YAKKING** about different food groups to poor bored Tiny Tim. And the poor bored audience. "A balanced diet is made up of the five food groups," she lectured.

"1. Protein.

2. Fruit and vegetables . . ."

Horrid Henry *yawned*. He could see the theatre critic asleep in the front

row. Better wake him up, thought
Henry. After all, the storm must still
be going on.

Horrid Henry pressed the
Thunderstorm button.

**BANG BANG BANG
BOOM BOOM BOOM**

The critic woke up and *scribbled*
furiously in his notebook.

The Good Food Fairy droned on.

Horrid Henry felt his eyelids droop. What a **DULL** play. If only he, Henry, had written this play, it would have been so much more exciting. He'd have had **TERMINATOR GLADIATOR** challenge the *Good Food Fairy* to a duel for a start, then—

"Sound effect!" *hissed* Miss Battle-Axe.

YIKES, thought Horrid Henry. Which sound effect?

Horrid Henry had no idea. He *jabbed* at the sound board.

MOOOOOOOO!

The audience laughed.

OOPS. Hadn't they met the cow
yet? He vaguely remembered that
Tiny Tim tripped over a cow at some
point.

"**I SAID,** THE GOOD FOOD FAIRY
HAS LANDED ON HER DAINTY FEET," yelled
Margaret, as the ear-splitting
MOOing continued.

Horrid Henry quickly took his
finger off the *Moo* button.

Dainty feet. Dainty feet? Didn't
someone break a foot because they

hadn't eaten enough calcium?

Horrid Henry pressed the

Cracking Bones button.

CRUNCH! CRACK!
CRUNCH! CRACK!

"Who's coming with us to the

future?" shouted the *Good Food Fairy*,

trying to be heard over the sound

of breaking bones.

"Why, it's Mr

Vitamin! Hello,

Mr Vitamin."

Weepy William crept

on to the stage.

He looked terrified.

There was a **TERRIBLE** silence.

"**SOUND EFFECT!**" *hissed* Miss Battle-Axe again.

Mr Vitamin? Who on earth was Mr Vitamin? thought Henry. Was he a **turkey**? There was a **turkey** in the play somewhere. Henry was sure someone had said **turkey**. He pressed the button.

Gobble gobble gobble, gobble gobble gobble.

"I said, 'Hello, Mr Vitamin'," repeated Margaret, glaring.

Gobble gobble gobble, gobble gobble gobble.

"MR VITAMIN," screeched Margaret. "Tiny Tim's *CAT*."

Cat? thought Henry. Boring! He should be a **DINOSAUR**. This stupid play would be so much better if he were a **DINOSAUR**.

Horrid Henry pressed the button.

ROARRRRRRRR!

Weepy William opened his mouth and then closed it. He'd obviously forgotten his line.

Better help him, thought Horrid Henry.

RING RING. RING RING.

"That's a Victorian phone," shouted Henry from the wings. "Why don't you answer it, Mr Vitamin?"

William didn't move.

VROOM! VROOM! VROOM! VROOM!

"Look, it's a spaceship, Mr Vitamin," shouted Henry. "Hop aboard."

"Waaaaaaaaaa," wailed Weepy William. "I forgot my line."

"And now I must leave you," yelled the **Good Food Fairy**. "But before I go I must—"

A terrible fart noise blasted out.

PPPRRRRRRFFTTTTTT!

The audience howled.

Horrid Henry beamed. After all, someone had to save the show.

Horrid Henry skipped home. He'd done it! Miss Battle-Axe had refused to give him his **Entertainer** badge until she read the critic's review the next day, which ended: *"The sound effects stole the show, turning what could have been a tedious play into a comedy tour de force. I hope we see many future performances of THE GOOD FOOD FAIRY."*

Henry had no idea what a *tour de force* was, but it must have been good because **MISS BATTLE-AXE** handed him his **Entertainer** badge straight afterwards.

"**ZOOM OF DOOM**, here I come!" whooped Horrid Henry.

HORRID
HENRY
AND THE ZOOM
OF DOOM

BOB BOB BOB BOB BOB.

The giant teacups bobbed down the lazy river.

"*Wheeeeeeee*," squealed Perfect Peter.

"*Wheeeeeeee*," squealed Tidy Ted.

"*Wheeeeeeee*," squealed Perky Parveen.

"*Wheeeeeeee!*" squealed all the mini ninnies seated in the giant floating teacups.

~~TERRIFIED SCREAMS~~ rang out from a nearby ride. Moody Margaret and Sour Susan and Brainy Brian and Jazzy Jim were *whizzing* down **Belly Flop Drop** in a **bouncing** rubber raft

which twisted and looped and spun
backwards.

"**DUCK**," hissed Henry. "Don't let
them see us."

Horrid Henry and **RUDE RALPH**
slunk down in their little seats as
low as they could. If Margaret or any
of their classmates saw them riding
in the *toddler teacups*, their names would

be **MUD** for ever.

"Sit up, Henry," said Miss Battle-Axe. "You too, Ralph."

Horrid Henry groaned.

How had he, Horrid Henry, ended up trapped in a giant teacup with **MISS BATTLE-AXE** and his *wormy worm* brother and the rest of *Miss Lovely's* infant class at **WILD WATER-SLIDE PARK**? He wanted to go racing down the **ZOOM OF DOOM**, the TWISTING, *LOOPING*, rollercoaster waterslide with the world's **STEEPEST** drop. Where cannonballs blasted you as you hurtled backwards through waterfalls, flipping you upside down and spinning you as you crashed **SCREAMING** into Crocodile Creek. Or **Belly Flop Drop**, with its jet sprays and stomach-churning twists. Or **CRASH SPLASH**, where rubber rings raced towards each other before veering off into **TUNNELS OF TERROR**.

The shame. The misery. The horror of being trapped in giant *teacups* instead. With — oh **WOE** — only more *baby* rides to come.

It was so unfair. He'd worked his **fingers** to the **bone** earning all those badges.

Was it his fault he'd disappeared with RUDE RALPH on the last class trip? The class had got lost, not them. Or that he'd jumped from the little white train **chugging** around the Second World War airfield on the school trip before that, because he'd seen a plane he needed to investigate?

That certainly wasn't his fault — it was the school's, for not showing them anything interesting.

"Gondola ride on the Baby Bayou next, everyone," smiled *Miss Lovely*.

"*Yay*," trilled the infants.

"The gondolas are *so exciting*," said Goody-Goody Gordon.

"I don't want to go on the stupid gondola ride!" yelled Horrid Henry. "I want to go on the **ZOOM OF DOOM!!**"

"That's much too scary," said Perfect Peter.

"It's a straight drop to the bottom," GASPED Tidy Ted.

"I'm scared of heights," whimpered Perky Parveen.

"Don't worry, we won't be going anywhere near the **ZOOM OF DOOM**," said *Miss Lovely*.

"I want to go on the **ZOOM OF DOOM!**" howled Horrid Henry.

"Henry. Ralph. You're staying with me," said **MISS BATTLE-AXE.** "And that's final. There will be no repeat of last year. Or the year before that. And as I **DO NOT LIKE** water slides, we will be sticking with *Miss Lovely's* class."

"**NOOOOOOOOOOOO!**" howled Horrid Henry.

"**NOOOOOOOOOOOO!**" howled Rude Ralph.

"**YES**," snapped **MISS BATTLE-AXE**. She shuddered. *UGGHH*. She would rather swim with **SHARKS** than go on a water slide and be hurled backwards into an abyss. The very thought made her feel faint. Once when she was a little girl she'd tried a *teeny weeny* rollercoaster and spent a week recovering from the fright in

a darkened
room. No water
slides for her.

Horrid Henry scowled. He had
to escape from Miss Battle-Axe and
get on the **ZOOM OF DOOM**. He had
to. He loved **scary rides** and **BIG
DROPS** and **ROLLERCOASTERS** more
than **ANYTHING** in the whole wide
world. The *TWISTIER*, the **TURNIER**,
the more *terrifying* the better. And
— oh, the **AGONY** — here he was, finally,
at **WILD WATER-SLIDE PARK**, and he
was trapped with the infants.

He whispered to **RUDE RALPH**.

Ralph smiled.

"Good plan," he said.

Just as their giant teacup reached
the dock, **RUDE RALPH** stood up,
wobbled and *toppled* over the side into
the river. He started **splashing**
and **SHRIEKING**.

"Man overboard!" shouted Horrid

Henry. "**HELP! HELP!**" He'd escape in all the commotion and get straight on the **ZOOM OF DOOM** before anyone could stop him.

Henry leapt off the teacup.

A **hideous** hand grabbed his shoulder.

"Not so fast," said **MISS BATTLE-AXE**.

"Why aren't you rescuing Ralph?" screamed Henry. "He's drowning."

"**HELP!**" yelped Ralph, **SPLUTTERING** and **FLAILING**. "**HELP!**"

"Stand up, Ralph," said **MISS BATTLE-AXE**. "Now."

Slowly, **RUDE RALPH** stood up in the shallow water, which only reached his knees.

R̶A̶T̶S̶.

"Everyone get in line and follow me to the Baby Bayou," trilled *Miss Lovely*.

"Yay," said Perfect Peter. "The Baby Bayou is my favourite ride."

Horrid Henry pinched Peter.

Perfect Peter screamed.

"Henry pinched me!" he wailed.

"I was just checking to see if you were an **alien**," *hissed* Henry. "And you are."

Moody Margaret and Sour Susan strolled past, laughing.

"Oh wow, that was so much fun," *squealed* Moody Margaret.

"Yeah," *squealed* Sour Susan.

"Let's go on the **ZOOM OF DOOM** now," said Margaret loudly. "And then **Belly Flop Drop** again."

"Yeah," said Sour Susan.

"Did you enjoy the giant teacups, Henry? I hope you weren't too

123

scared," said Moody Margaret,
smirking.

Horrid Henry gritted his teeth.

What could he say? Or do? Other
than hope that a **GIANT SEA MONSTER**
would rise up from the Lazy River
and swallow Margaret whole.

"Too bad you won't get to ride the **ZOOM OF DOOM**, Henry," said Margaret.

"**NAH NAH NE NAH NAH**," jeered Margaret and Susan, racing off to join the long queue snaking away from the entrance to the **ZOOM OF DOOM**.

"We've got to escape," muttered Horrid Henry.

"Too right," said **RUDE RALPH**.

Henry looked at Ralph.

Ralph looked at Henry.

"Run!" shouted **Horrid Henry**.

Henry and Ralph ran off as fast as they could. They darted through the crowds, *pushing* and **shoving** and **LEAPING**, closer and closer to the **ZOOM OF D—**

CRASH! BANG!

"And where do you think you're going?" came a **TERRIBLE** voice.

Huh?

There was **MISS BATTLE-AXE** standing in front of them, arms crossed. They'd slammed right into her.

"We needed the loo," said Henry.

"It was an emergency," said **RUDE RALPH**.

MISS BATTLE-AXE glared at them.

"If you so much as move an **INCH** from my side again, you will be taken straight to the **BAD CHILDREN'S ROOM** to wait for your parents to collect you," said Miss Battle-Axe.

Yikes.

THE BAD CHILDREN'S ROOM.

If Henry got sent home he'd have **NO** chance of ever getting on the **ZOOM OF DOOM**. His parents would never take him back to **WILD**

WATER-SLIDE PARK, that was for sure.

He'd have to grit his teeth and find another way.

Horrid Henry and Rude Ralph followed the infants to the gondolas on the Baby Bayou.

"I feel **SEASICK,**" said RUDE RALPH suddenly. "Those teacups made me dizzy. I need to go to the First Aid room." He **belched** loudly, then WINKED at Henry.

"**ohhhh!** Yeah, me too," said Horrid Henry. He clutched his stomach. "**OWW. oWWWW.** You can just leave

130

us to recover there," he moaned. "We don't want to stop anyone having fun."

Miss Battle-Axe took **Horrid Henry** and **RUDE RALPH**, groaning and moaning, to the First Aid room.

They lay down on two cots.

"No need to stay with us," **GROANED** Henry.

"We'll just lie here till it's home time," **MOANED** Ralph.

"These boys are suffering from seasickness," said **MISS BATTLE-AXE** to the nurse.

"Tummy ache?" said the nurse.

"Yes," moaned Henry.

"Dizzy?"

"Oh yes," said Ralph.

"Feeling like you are going to vomit?"

"Any second," said Henry.

"Not to worry," said the nurse.

"I have just the right injection." She advanced towards them, waving two **ENORMOUS** needles.

"You know, I feel a lot better," said Henry, sitting up.

"Me too," said Ralph.

"Excellent," said **MISS BATTLE-AXE**. "Now off we go to the **Dozy Dinghies**. If we're lucky, we'll catch *Miss Lovely* at the steamboats for a relaxing journey around the Pixie Pond."

How was it possible, thought Henry miserably, trudging after her, to have so many baby rides in a water-slide park?

He could see Tough Toby and Fiery Fiona whizzing down **PANIC PRECIPICE**, whooping and laughing while he was trapped on the *Pixie Pond*.

"Last ride before home time," said *Miss Lovely*. "*Lullaby Lagoon* or the *Fairy Float Boats*?"

"*Lullaby Lagoon* might be too scary," said Spotless Sam.

"How about the **CANNIBAL CANOES**, where you get eaten as you ride?" snarled **Horrid Henry**. "That's why all the canoes come back empty."

"Quiet, Henry," said **MISS BATTLE-AXE**. Soon, she'd be safely home, with her feet up, and the school outing would

be over for another year.

"*Fairy Floats, Fairy Floats*," chanted the infants.

"Where are the *Fairy Float Boats*?" said *Miss Lovely*. Miss Battle-Axe consulted her map.

"Right next to the **ZOOM OF DOOM**," said **MISS BATTLE-AXE**, pointing to the huge queues jostling each other waiting for both rides.

Just to torture him, thought **Horrid Henry** as he plodded over to the queue for the *Fairy Float Boats.* Could his day have got even worse?

So near, and yet so far.

There were so many people *pushing* and **SHOVING** that the queues were starting to mix. You couldn't tell which queue was which.

And then Horrid Henry had a *brilliant*, **SPECTACULAR** idea. It was **perilous.** It was **DANGEROUS.** The chance of success was *tiny*. And yet . . . and yet . . . how could he not risk his life for a chance to ride the **ZOOM OF DOOM**?

"Come on, everyone, this way, this way," said Henry, weaving through

the **MASSIVE** queues. Perfect Peter, Goody-Goody Gordon and Tidy Ted followed him.

Slowly, Henry *inched* his way to the right into the **ZOOM OF DOOM** queue.

"Follow me," shouted **RUDE RALPH**, ushering **MISS BATTLE-AXE**, *Miss Lovely* and her class to the right behind Henry.

Finally they reached the head of the queue.

"What's this ride again?" asked Perky Parveen.

"*Fairy Float Boats*," said Henry,

grabbing a seat at the front of the **BLACK SKULL** raft.

"Oh, I love the Fairy Float Boats," said Perfect Peter.

Miss Lovely and **MISS BATTLE-AXE** sat down.

"I don't remember seat belts on the Fairy Float Boats," said Miss Battle-Axe, buckling up. "Do you, Lydia?"

"No," said Miss Lovely. "Must be new HEALTH AND SAFETY rules. Seat belts on, everyone."

The rubber rafts began a slow ascent up the track.

"Lydia," said Miss Battle-Axe. "I don't remember riding in **BLACK SKULLS** on the *Fairy Float Boats*, do you?"

"Must be a new design," said Miss Lovely.

The rafts climbed higher. Soft music began to play.

"Boudicca," said *Miss Lovely*, "don't we seem rather high up for the *Fairy Float Boats* . . ."

"Now that you mention it," said Miss Battle-Axe. She peered over the edge. "Lydia, I've got the feeling we're not—"

But before she could finish speaking

139

the raft PLUNGED over the edge, SPUN
BACKWARDS and PLUMMETED straight down.
MISS BATTLE-AXE screamed.

"AAAAARRRGGGGHHHIIE"

Miss Lovely screamed.
The infants screamed.

"WHOOPEEEEE!"
shrieked Henry and Ralph.
They'd done it. They were
riding on the ZOOM OF DOOM
at last.
Life was sweet.

FRANCESCA SIMON

FRANCESCA SIMON SPENT HER CHILDHOOD ON THE BEACH IN CALIFORNIA
AND STARTED WRITING STORIES AT THE AGE OF EIGHT. SHE WROTE HER
FIRST HORRID HENRY BOOK IN 1994. HORRID HENRY HAS GONE ON TO
CONQUER THE GLOBE; HIS ADVENTURES HAVE SOLD MILLIONS OF COPIES
WORLDWIDE.

FRANCESCA HAS WON THE CHILDREN'S BOOK OF THE YEAR AWARD AND IN
2009 WAS AWARDED A GOLD BLUE PETER BADGE. SHE WAS ALSO A TRUSTEE
OF THE WORLD BOOK DAY CHARITY FOR SIX YEARS.

FRANCESCA LIVES IN NORTH LONDON WITH HER FAMILY.

WWW.FRANCESCASIMON.COM
WWW.HORRIDHENRY.CO.UK
@SIMON_FRANCESCA

TONY ROSS

TONY ROSS WAS BORN IN LONDON AND STUDIED AT THE LIVERPOOL SCHOOL OF ART AND DESIGN. HE HAS WORKED AS A CARTOONIST, A GRAPHIC DESIGNER, AN ADVERTISING ART DIRECTOR AND A UNIVERSITY LECTURER.

TONY IS ONE OF THE MOST POPULAR AND SUCCESSFUL CHILDREN'S ILLUSTRATORS OF ALL TIME, BEST KNOWN FOR ILLUSTRATING HORRID HENRY AND THE WORKS OF DAVID WALLIAMS, AS WELL AS HIS OWN HUGELY POPULAR SERIES, THE LITTLE PRINCESS. HE LIVES IN MACCLESFIELD.

COLLECT ALL THE
HORRID HENRY STORYBOOKS!